Spellbound Books

presents

Eat Your Own Brain

GW00640690

A COLLECTION OF SHORT STORIES
By
Mike Russell

I.S.B.N: 0-9541097-1-6

Contents

8.The Meeting

12.Dunce

16.The Invention

17.The End Of The Milkman

20.Mask Man

26.The Diaries Of Sun City

30.Terry Takes A Dip

31.The Exit to Vince's Voyeurs' Emporium

33.Everything Is Fine

36.Up!

39.Brad's Quest

43.The Miracle

48.Wooden Globe

49.Love On The Other Side

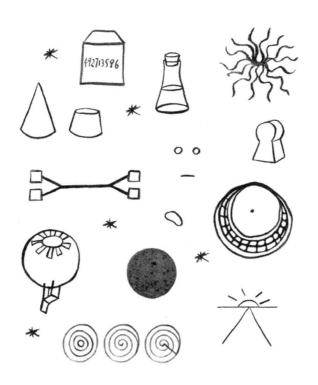

The Meeting

Two detached houses stand side by side. They are both built from the local stone. One is painted red and one is painted blue. A path, also constructed from the local stone but left unpainted, leads from the door of each house. The two paths meet twenty-five metres from the doors and become one. This single path continues for fifty metres then divides into two again. These two paths continue each for another twenty-five metres then stop at two doors of two different buildings; both made from the local stone. One is painted red and one is painted blue. These two buildings are different from the two houses. The houses have pointed roofs and windows front and back; the other two buildings are half as high with flat roofs and no windows.

Apart from these four buildings and the paths between them there is nothing but grass, neatly mown, as far as I can see. It has always been like this.

I live in the red house. I have always lived there. The house is well furnished. In exchange for these comforts I work in the red building.

The red building contains a single room, which is painted the same red as the building's exterior. I stand upon two black silhouettes of feet printed on the floor. In front of me, in the centre of the room, is a red plinth. On top of the plinth, in its centre, is a round, red button. Behind the plinth, set into the floor, is a metal grill. On the far wall is a dial. It is this dial that I watch, with my hand hovering above the button. The hand of the dial is turning round. At the top of the dial is a small red arrow that points down. The hand turns round. It now points at the arrow. I press the button. Nothing happens. The hand continues to turn until it points at the arrow again. I press the button. Nothing happens. Life goes by.

Life is fine except for the headaches. Every morning I awake with a pain in the centre of my forehead. Pain hurts. This, at least, I have learnt. The pain makes it difficult for me to raise my head and when standing it forces me to stare at the ground. As the day progresses the pain fades but the next morning it returns just as before.

The hand of the dial reaches the arrow and stops. It is time to leave. I turn around, unhook my coat from the back of the door, leave the building and begin to lock the door. The locking of the door is an elaborate procedure involving keys, bolts and combinations. It takes some time. When it is done I turn around and begin to walk down the path towards the red house.

The sky is clear, the grass is lush. I walk along the path. I cannot see her yet. Now I can. She is tiny but she is growing larger as her footsteps grow louder. Now I can see her clearly but I cannot see her face because she is looking at the ground. We pass each other every evening. Her head is always hanging down. We also pass each other every morning but then of course it is *my* head that hangs because of the pain. Consequently I have never seen her face. It is a mystery to me. It is a blur in a sharply focused world.

It is the next morning. I awake. The pain is in the exact centre of my forehead as usual. I sit up, staring at the bed, unable to lift my head. I stand up, I wash, I dress, I breakfast, I leave the house. I walk along the path towards the red building, my head still hanging. I hear her footsteps grow louder and louder then quieten and disappear. I enter the building. I stand upon the footprints. The dial's hand begins to turn. It reaches the arrow. I press the button. Life goes by.

I leave the red building, the pain now gone and walk, with my head up, along the path. She grows as she nears. Her head is hanging down. We pass each other. It is almost certain that she lives in the blue house and it is almost certain that she works in the blue building. She almost certainly works nights.

It is the next morning. I am walking to work. My head hangs. I hear her footsteps. I hear them grow louder. Something has been wrong for a long time. Something has been missing from my world. There are questions that have never been asked. Is something changing? I cannot explain but there are questions and desires that are stronger than the pain in my head and my neck is slowly straightening. Is it possible that she only hangs her head in the evenings? I want to see her face. I push through the pain. Her head is not hanging down. I see her face. How can I describe her visage? A list of observations would be profoundly insufficient. It is better to say that seeing it renders the rest of the world indistinct.

9

"Morning", she says.

"Morning", I say, "I expected you to say 'evening'. You work nights don't you? In the blue building?"

"Yes. My evenings are your mornings. I am on my way home."

"You always hang your head in the evenings, my evenings, your mornings."

"Yes, I suffer from headaches every morning", she says, "I always awake with a pain just here", she points at the centre of her forehead. I look at her, shocked.

"You always hang your head in the evenings, my evenings, your mornings", she says.

"Yes, well, I must get to work", I say, "See you this evening".

"Yes, see you in the morning".

How different everything now seems. I walk on, then enter the red building. Life goes by.

I walk towards her down the path. Her head is hanging but as we reach each other she slowly raises her neck through her pain and looks at me. Knowing that pain, I reach out and gently rest my hand upon her shoulder. Her face shows distress.

"I know what causes my headaches", she says.

I am shocked. I have never before thought that such a question could be asked. What causes the pain? I stare at her with anticipation.

"I didn't sleep last night, partly because the sun was shining bright through my curtains but also..." she pauses, "Because I was thinking about you. I was lying face up on my bed with my eyes open when suddenly a small hatch opened in the ceiling. I was so scared that I could not move. Then a small red hammer emerged on the end of a red rod, stopped just above my head then hit me in the centre of my forehead."

I stared at her, aghast.

"A few moments went by then it hit me again. It hit my forehead regularly until the morning then the rod retreated, pulling the hammer back inside the hole, then the hatch closed.

I can't talk anymore or I'll be late for work. I'm going to sleep on the floor tonight. See you."

She hurries past me.

I am scared. Life is very strange yet I have nothing to compare it to.

I am at home. I walk into my bedroom, stand on my bed and examine the ceiling. I find nothing to confirm or disprove my suspicions so I lay down and fall asleep.

It is morning and I awake without any pain. It is extraordinary. It has never happened before. Something is definitely happening. I leave the house and walk towards her with my head up. She looks very frightened. Before I can speak she says:

"I have something very strange to tell you. I have been thinking about my job..."

"What is it that you do?"

"I press a blue button. But I had never before considered what it might do. Isn't that insane? I just never thought that the question could be asked..."

I am sweating. What does the button do? Why have I never asked that? My life is being opened up. I am terrified.

"What does the button do?" I ask.

"The blue button is on top of a plinth. Behind the plinth is a metal grill set into the floor. I didn't press the button today; instead I lifted the metal grill, revealing a metal staircase which descended into darkness. I climbed down the steps into a dark room, found a light switch on the wall and pressed it. The room was the same size as the one above. A blue rod was protruding from the middle of the ceiling. It must lead from the blue button. The rod led down to the floor then bent at ninety degrees and travelled along the floor then disappeared into a hole in the wall. The opening was just big enough to crawl into. Holding onto the rod, I crawled into the darkness, through a long tunnel for about one hundred metres then eventually came up against a wall. The rod bent at ninety degrees and travelled up the wall, next to it was a ladder, which I climbed, still feeling the rod, which bent again at ninety degrees. The top of the wall was a floor. The rod continued for about a metre then disappeared into a square opening in the floor from which a dim light flooded. I peered through the opening."

She had been staring at the sky whilst speaking but now she stares at me for a moment with an expression of fear, confusion and trepidation then quickly looks away.

"What did you see?" I ask.

She draws breath.

"The end of the blue rod was attached to a small blue hammer which was hovering above a man's head whilst he slept in bed."

My jaw drops.

"It was too dark to see his face", she says quickly, urgently.

"So", I say, "There is someone out there who wakes up every morning with a pain in their head just like you and I bet they press a red button every day at work."

"Yes".

She casts around for words but remains silent, her mouth opens and closes on air.

"Will you kiss me please", I say.

Dunce

Everyone calls Dunce "Dunce". Dunce is dim. If he were a bulb he'd be black; he'd darken the brightest of rooms. Plug in a Dunce bulb and you'll be fumbling around and falling over furniture guaranteed. If Dunce were in that dark room himself though he'd have no problem finding his way because he's intuitive, you know?

Dunce is completely bald and he has a really pointed head so the temptation to get him paralytic on his thirtieth birthday, carry him to the tattooist's and get a nice big "D" smack bang in the middle of his forehead was too much for me. Trouble is he can't afford to have it removed so he wears a big plaster over it. Gangs of children tease him.

"What's underneath the plaster, mister? Show us!"
They swear that he has a third eye under there.

My name is Mustafa but Dunce calls me "Fez" on account of my hat. I've known Dunce for sixteen years, I don't have to use my memory to work that out; I just count the number of boxes of Turkish Delight I've got stashed in a cupboard and halve it. Dunce buys me a box every Christmas and birthday. Dunce thought that being Turkish I would like that powder-covered gunk. I hate the stuff.

On my last birthday I decided to take Dunce to the theatre. He'd never been before.

"No, Dunce, I'll eat them later", I said, quickly stashing box number thirty-two in the cupboard.

The play was called "Death in the Dark". We had front row seats. Dunce was captivated. He stared at the actors with a gaping mouth.

The lights dimmed to darkness. Kitty Malone, the beautiful star of the show, was stood centre stage. A shot was heard. Dunce jumped right out of his seat.

"What was that?" he said.

The lights came back on and Kitty was lying in a pool of blood. Dunce let out a scream then shouted:

"Someone call for an ambulance! And the police!"

The audience thought that Dunce was an actor, that the play was being cleverly extended beyond the stage, questioning the boundaries of theatre.

"What's wrong with you?" Dunce shouted at the audience. "How can you carry on as if nothing has happened!"

"This is wonderful, just wonderful", I heard someone say behind me.

Kitty was stoically sticking to her role, thinking that the show must go on, but Dunce was clambering up onto the stage, crying, stroking Kitty's hair and checking her pulse.

"She's alive!" he shouted.

"No I'm not!" Kitty hissed at him through clenched teeth.

That was it; I was in hysterics. What a birthday treat this was turning out to be.

"I'm acting. It's part of the play. No one really shot me", Kitty hissed at Dunce.

The realisation was excruciatingly slow. I watched Dunce's face change from shock to confusion to understanding to embarrassment. He made his way back to his seat. He didn't speak or look at me until the play was over. The play got a standing ovation and we headed for the bar.

Kitty was in the bar too. She smiled at Dunce who blushed. She seemed to be fascinated by the top of his head then she walked over and invited him to her dressing room.

Twelve hours later and Dunce was in love; how about that. And what's more, Kitty was in love too. And not only that but they were in love with each other. She fell for him. Not fell for as in was deceived by because there's no deception where Dunce is concerned, he can't do it, but she fell from her deceptions towards him. I couldn't believe it.

"It won't last", I said to Dunce. "Enjoy it while you can but face facts you are Dunce and she is Kitty Malone. Think about it."

Dunce told me that Kitty had a thing about ice cream cones, a fetish you could say. She ate three a day. She liked to bite off the tip of the cone and suck out all the ice cream. She had a tape-recording of ice cream van music that she played whilst they were having sex. She was forever stroking the top of Dunce's head. It made Dunce beam brighter than any bulb.

Then came the day. Dunce came round looking really worried.

"Fez, have you seen Kitty? Do you know where she is?"

"No, I haven't seen her. Why? What's the problem?"

"I had a dream last night. I was in bed and I looked at the calendar by the side of my bed and it was tonight. I put out my hand to touch Kitty but she wasn't there. There was just this cold sludge covering her side of the bed and this smell: vanilla. It was ice cream, melted ice cream."

"So what's the problem?"

"I think that something is going to happen to Kitty. I have to find her before tonight. I don't want to wake up tomorrow morning alone in a bed full of melted ice cream."

"Dunce, dreams are randomly produced by the brain in the absence of a rational conscious self. It is rationality that you need to employ in this situation and rationally it is unlikely that what you experienced was a prophecy. Sit yourself down. Let's have a couple of beers."

I opened a cupboard, reached in to get the beers and a pile of boxes of Turkish Delight toppled and fell, breaking open and spilling their contents all over the floor. Dunce looked at the boxes then looked at me. I watched his face go through the same slow transformation from shock to confusion to understanding to embarrassment that I had witnessed so many times before.

"You don't like Turkish Delight?" he said.

I said nothing and guiltily handed him a beer.

Dunce sighed then said:

"So why did I have that dream?"

"No reason at all", I said then explained more about the brain's functioning during sleep.

Dunce suddenly stood up.

"It's no good, Fez, I have to find her."

Dunce found Kitty in the centre of town, lying on the pavement in a pool of blood. An ambulance and the police were on their way. An ice cream vendor was crying and yelling:

"I don't understand! I don't understand!"

A huge plastic ice cream cone was protruding from Kitty's chest. It had fallen from on top of the ice cream shop for no apparent reason, smashed through her rib cage and crushed her heart.

Dunce cried, then he cried some more. The next day he cried and the day after that he cried. Three weeks later he awoke, dressed, ate some breakfast then cried. The next day he came round to see me. He was crying.

"Hello Dunce", I said, "Do you want a beer?"

"What's wrong with you?" he said. "How can you carry on as if nothing has happened?"

"It was an accident, Dunce"; I said angrily, "A random occurrence. These things happen. You just have to get on with life. Why are you so stupid?"

14

I regretted saying it as soon as I heard it come out of my mouth. Dunce stared at me with tears in his eyes.

"A fez is only a severed cone. At least I have a point", Dunce said.

I took off my hat and looked at it sullenly. Dunce had a point that he had a point. If he'd found Kitty a moment earlier... if I hadn't delayed him with my arrogance...

"Fez, you remember the tears that I cried in the theatre when I thought that Kitty was dead but she wasn't. I think that the tears that I am crying now are the same as those. I didn't understand what was going on in the theatre and I didn't understand what was going on when the cone fell on her. I think that maybe we only cry because we don't understand what is going on", Dunce said, "Maybe if we understood what is really going on we wouldn't cry at all, ever", Dunce smiled through his tears, and beneath the plaster on his forehead I thought I saw something move.

The Invention

"I dreamt deeply last night..." he says.

He is holding his right hand out in front of him, clenched into a fist. His other hand is cupped over the fist protectively as if something delicate and precious dwells within.

His eyes are wide; his pupils are massive.

"You may want to sit down."

You sit down and he takes the cupped hand away from the fist then the fingers slowly open and there it is, resting on the palm (or is it hovering?): a small, dark, hollow object containing a gyrating red bean. What is it?

"I knew exactly how to make it as soon as I awoke but now I can't remember how I made it or what it is for. It makes no sense."

You wonder about his sanity but he is as bemused and as scared as you. He continues to be as conventional as he has always been and no similar incidents occur yet the existence of the dark, hollow object and its continually gyrating red bean cannot be denied. It sits on a shelf in the corner of the room whilst we watch "Eastenders".

The End Of The Milkman

It took a long time to start the milk float. In between distributing the bottles on the doorsteps he tried to will the vehicle to move a little faster, for in his white uniform's jacket-pocket was a fixed future appointment that he did not want to miss, but the vehicle's speed was constant and he had to wait. He had to believe that the appointment would be kept, that his hope would materialise. He felt the train-ticket through the fabric of his jacket whilst the milk float trundled on.

He finished his round then ran from the dairy to his house. Running made up for the time which had been lost whilst trying to start the milk float and also gave him time to spare before he had to leave for the train-station. He sat in an armchair, holding the ticket and looking at the clock on the wall.

His wife lay in a bed in a hospital.

"There will be an end to this pain", she thought, "I see a thread stretching away from me into the distance but I do not see its end. I am travelling towards the horizon so the end of the thread must draw closer, surely. Or does the thread stretch right around the world? Have I been here before? No, no, there must be an end."

"All in good time" said the voices around the bed.

"Why did he steal the cow?" she thought.

"All in good time".

"She will get better", the milkman thought, "I will see her again. I will be able to explain."

The milkman and his wife had argued about the cow then she had left the house, slamming the door behind her then he had received a phone-call saying that she was in hospital.

The milkman looked through the window at the cow grazing in the garden under the branch-less tree, ran his fingers through his hair then stood up and walked into the kitchen. He opened the refrigerator, which was full of bottles of milk, removed one, indented the foil top, lifted the bottle then drank until it was empty. He placed the empty bottle on top of the refrigerator then returned to the sitting room and looked at the clock. It was time to leave.

He walked towards the station, clutching his ticket in his hand.

He had written a letter in the morning, in between receiving the phone-call and beginning his round, in case the first-class post was collected and delivered faster than he could travel to the hospital. He had written the letter using the paper and charcoal that he and his wife had made on their anniversary from the branches of the

17

tree that they had planted on their wedding day. He would never have believed when they had planted the tree that it would turn into this. The letter read:

"I am coming to see you. I hope you are all right. Derek was wrong. He was lying. I did not steal the cow from the dairy; I bought it. You must know this."

He had placed the letter in an envelope, sealed, addressed and stamped it then posted it into a red pillar-box. The letter had entered the cylinder of darkness and waited.

Fields passed by the window as the train's wheels turned around on the tracks. The seats in the carriage were decorated with circles. The milkman stared out of the window and listened to the other travellers speaking:

"Turn to the last page Mum, come on, come on."

"The fastest way to travel from point A to point B is to fold space, to bring point A and point B together."

"If only the parallel tracks of the railway would meet, if only I could stand on the horizon", the milkman thought.

Then suddenly the train had arrived. The milkman ran through the station, across the street and into the hospital, found the ward, found the bed but she was not there. He found a nurse and the nurse said:

"I am sorry, she is dead."

"But I have something that I have to tell her", he said.

"Now I am here and she is not here. How to bridge the gap?" the milkman thought.

He awoke the next morning in a cold bed. He sat up. His hair remained on the pillow. He stumbled into the bathroom and stared at his bald head in the mirror then stumbled back into the bedroom and stared at his hair on the pillow.

"I look like a baby now", he thought, "All the hair that separated the man from the child is gone. I am glad, for I am sick of all these divisions, these boundaries."

He cast his eyes around for his milkman's uniform, found it and ripped each garment to shreds. He strode into the kitchen, picked up the empty milk-bottle from on top of the refrigerator and threw it at the floor where it smashed. He turned around, opened the back door, walked towards the cow, got down onto his hands and knees, took its udder in his hands and drank.

"I want no more divisions", he thought, "I want to head for infinity where parallel lines meet."

Mask Man

Tom wants to shout but he does not want to wake Millie who is lying next to him. The pain fills all of his body.

"Is this pain me?" he thinks.

Sometimes Tom is more aware of the pain than at other times. Earlier this evening for example, whilst Millie was kissing him, he was not even aware that such a thing as pain existed.

Tom does not know the name of his pain or the name of its' cause. His doctor cannot explain it. The pain appeared last winter. Tom cannot pinpoint the exact moment but surely there must have been one: a moment between feeling fine and having a tiny amount of pain.

"Did the pain's cause malevolently possess me or did I invite it in?" he thinks, "I do not know. Sometimes one has a thought and it cannot be obliterated; it can be ignored or entertained but not obliterated. It becomes a door: a polished wooden door with a polished wooden handle. Did the illness slip through such an opening? Where do such thoughts come from?"

Tom hides the pain. No one else but his doctor knows about it. He especially hides it from Millie. He does not want her smile to fade. His face is a mask that hides the pain. Her face is like glass. Tom looks at Millie now and even asleep her lips are slightly smiling. He whispers:

"Oh, sleep take me to that truth. Let me be glass."

"It's the fancy dress party at the weekend, Tom, you should think about what you're going to go as," says Millie.

"What are you going to go as?" Tom asks.

"A nurse."

"Why a nurse?"

"I've always wanted to be one."

Tom has bought some clay. He sits at his dressing table and kneads it. He wants to make a mask. He looks hard at the clay. The more he stares at it the more he becomes aware of the pain until it becomes unbearable. He stands up and walks around the room, thinking about Millie's smile. Feeling a little better, he confronts the clay once more. Again his awareness of the pain grows the more he stares at the clay. With painful hands he begins to mould the material. He does not think about the clay, he thinks about the pain, the way it feels, its particular... physiognomy. The clay begins to take the form of a face. The face becomes more defined. He smoothes its surface, holds it at arms length and levels his gaze at its unseeing eyes.

"This is the face of the pain," he thinks.

He pushes a skewer through each of its pupils then through each of its nostrils, he then makes two holes at the sides for elastic, and one in the centre of the mouth, then puts the mask in the oven and turns up the heat.

When it is hard, dry and cool he paints the mask red, attaches a length of elastic then tries it on in front of the mirror.

"This mask does not hide, it reveals," he thinks, "The pain has a face."

"What are you going as, Tom?"

"I'm going as someone else."

Millie laughs.

"Oh, Millie!"

"You like it, huh?"

"You look fabulous!"

"Oh, so you have a nurse thing, huh?"

"I guess, I mean I maybe, I don't know, err..."

Millie kisses Tom's cheek.

"You look nice in your suit. Put your mask on," she says.

"Wow! You're scary!" she laughs then kisses the mask on the cheek.

"Don't do that!" Tom shouts.

Millie backs off.

"Sorry", Tom says, "I didn't mean to shout. I didn't like that. Sorry. I don't know why. Sorry."

Millie frowns.

"OK," she says.

It is dark as Tom and Millie walk hand in hand through the town. It feels good to Tom to be wearing the mask and holding Nurse Millie's hand.

They arrive at the door to the party. Millie knocks. The door opens.

"Hi Millie, nice outfit," says a woman with whiskers, pointed ears and a tail.

"Hello," Tom says, "I'm Tom," and holds out his hand. The cat woman looks at him and her smile fades. She says nothing.

"This is Tom," Millie repeats, "My husband."

"Yes. Yes, hello Tom. Sorry. It's just... I don't know whether Richard will see the funny side. Perhaps you know him better than I do. Come in anyway. Come in."

She stands aside, Millie and Tom exchange a confused glance then they enter.

The room is huge and full of people in costumes chatting and drinking.

"Who's Richard?" Tom asks Millie.

"I don't know. Let's not stay long. I've got a bad feeling about this."

"Yes, I know what you mean."

Tom picks up two glasses of red wine and hands one to Millie who is chatting to another nurse; they compare each other's outfits.

An Egyptian mummy walks towards Tom and holds up his bandaged hands.

"Let there be music!" the mummy shouts.

Three small men with seemingly decaying flesh clamber up onto a table and begin to sing in close harmony:

"A song of glass,
A song of glass,
A song of glass,
A song of glass,
A song of glass..."

The tune repeats around and around then fades.

Tom is the first to applaud and the last to stop.

"Wonderful," Tom says to the mummy.

"You look like you could do with something stronger than that," the mummy says, pointing at Tom's drink, "I know *I* could. There is somewhere we could go."

"I can't leave. I'm with my wife."

"It's just another room. This is my party."

"Oh! It's a great place you've got here."

"I moved into this house last winter."

Tom follows the mummy out of the room. Millie is still chatting to the nurse.

The mummy leads Tom through a corridor lined with red baroque wallpaper. At the end of the corridor is a polished wooden door with a polished wooden handle. They enter through the door into a small room covered in the same red wallpaper. An ornately framed oval mirror hangs on the far wall. In the centre of the room is a square polished wooden table and two polished wooden chairs. On the table are a white china plate and a silver knife and fork set for a meal.

"So what is it? I've tried most things," Tom says to the mummy.

The mummy does not answer. He sits in the chair that faces the plate and cutlery.

Beneath the mirror is a polished wooden fluted plinth with a petri dish on top of it. Tom walks over to the plinth and peers at the dish's contents. Some kind of fungus is growing in the dish.

"What is this? Some sort of disease?" Tom asks.

"Sit down," says the mummy.

Tom sits down opposite the mummy who looks at Tom for some time without saying anything then takes hold of one of the bandages wrapped around his head, pulls it loose and begins to unwind it, eventually revealing a face that is inflamed red and raw.

The face looks exactly like Tom's mask.

"Oh God," Tom says, shocked. He takes off his mask and places it on the table; "I had no idea. This is a coincidence, a strange coincidence. I assure you I have never seen you before…I don't know what to say."

The man stares intently at Tom's face then says:

"My name is Richard."

At that moment the door opens and a woman enters dressed in high leather boots, straps, buckles and studs.

"Hi Ricky", she says, draping her arm around Richard's neck and kissing his face.

"Is this woman in love with my pain?" Tom thinks.

"Later," Richard says and the woman reluctantly leaves, scowling at Tom as she does so.

When the door has closed Richard unwinds the rest of his bandages, underneath which he is wearing an identical suit to Tom's.

"Wait for me here," he says then leaves the room.

Tom picks the mask up, puts it back on, stands up and looks at himself in the mirror.

Richard returns to the party. Millie ambles drunkenly towards him.

"Hello Tom, I thought I'd lost you," she says.

The polished wooden door opens and the woman in bondage gear enters and leers at Tom.

"Let's dance," she says.

"But there's no music."

"So?"

She puts her arms around Tom's neck and begins to sway. Then she presses her lips against Tom's ear and whispers:

"Tell me how much it hurts, baby. Are you hurting now, hmm? Are you, honey? Is it agony?"

One of her hands moves from around Tom's neck and starts moving between her legs.

Tom removes her other arm from around him and steps back, against the plinth. The woman looks at Tom quizzically.

"I thought you were going to dress up."

She steps forward and kisses the mask.

"Don't! Please don't do that."

"Oh, but I like to do that. Tell me how much it hurts."

She kisses it again.

"What's this?" she says and pulls at the mask's elastic. It comes undone and the mask falls to the floor. The woman screams then picks the mask up. She looks at it and screams again.

"Richard!" she shouts.

She kisses the mask all over then falls to her knees in front of the plinth, bowing down to the disease.

"Richard, Richard," she weeps, tears running down her face to fall upon the mask.

"Millie, I have a secret to tell you," Richard says.

"Oh good, I like secrets," Millie says.

"I am in constant pain."

"What?" Millie stares at Richard, "Since when?"

"Last winter."

"Why?"

"I don't know."

"Why didn't you tell me?"

Richard does not answer.

"Oh Tom, my poor darling," Millie's smile fades. She wraps her arms around Richard's neck and kisses his cheek. Richard feels hollow, and he feels that it is the empty space within him that Millie is kissing. She kisses him again.

"Please, I don't like that."

"Sorry darling, I forgot. Take your mask off so I can kiss you properly."

"I wish I could."

Richard turns around and walks through the partying crowd and out of the room.

"Where are you going? Tom? Tom!" Millie calls.

Richard returns to the small room and sits back down opposite Tom. The woman jumps up from the floor and throws her arms around him.

"Richard, Richard," she cries, kissing his face.

Although the woman's kisses kiss Richard and not the empty space inside him, the thought that the space inside him exists can not be obliterated. It is unbearable.

"What now?" Tom says.

24

Richard stands up, picks up the mask, sits down again and places the mask on the china plate. The woman sits on the floor at Richard's side, then he picks up the fork, stabs it into the mask, picks up the knife, saws off a slice of the mask, stabs the slice with the fork, puts it in his mouth then swallows.

"That's clay," Tom says.

Richard ignores him and cuts off another slice. With every mouthful that Richard swallows Tom feels the pain within him decrease. Richard continues to eat the mask until the plate is empty, the space inside him is full and Tom feels no pain at all.

Tom is speechless.

"Lock the door on your way out," Richard says as he unties a key from around the woman's neck and hands it to Tom.

"Thankyou," Tom says, "Thankyou," then leaves the room, locks the door behind him and puts the key in his pocket.

Inside the room, behind the locked polished wooden door, Richard suddenly explodes into screams of agony. He smashes the china plate, breaks the mirror and breaks the chairs over the table. The woman sits in a corner, grinning and masturbating whilst Richard knocks over the plinth. He throws himself onto the floor, still yelling incomprehensibly, and eats the fungus out of the petri dish.

Tom walks towards Millie.

"I think maybe I *have* got a bit of a nurse thing," Tom says.

The Diaries Of Sun City

We live in a small city on a small world. The city is the only city; the world is the only world. The city is built in the shape of a sun. Its concrete rays house the living quarters; its circular centre is where we work and shop.

People write diaries for a particular reason here, where our social etiquette is constricting. These unwritten laws are self-imposed. They are born from fear. We are closed people. We creep around, suspicious of the changing skies.

Diaries are so popular that they have their own shop. It is called: "We Are Diaries". I have not owned a diary until now. The idea of placing my most secret, most sacred feelings out in the world terrifies me but I have bought a small black plastic bound book with blank, white pages and the word "Diary" embossed on the cover.

I walk through the city centre with the diary in my pocket and catch the bus that runs up and down the concrete ray that houses my flat. My flat is at the very end of the ray.

Inside my flat I sit facing the far wall, with the diary on my lap open at the first page. I write with pen and ink:

"Dear Diary,

Why can I not say it to her? It would be wrong to of course, inappropriate, rude in the extreme. She would be offended undoubtedly, that would be expected of her. Reluctantly her colleagues would be obliged to sever their relations with me; my associates would be informed, warned and, to avoid being chastised themselves, forced to sever their relations with me also. I would have to feel ashamed. Yet I would not. I would not be ashamed when talking to you dear Diary, I would be proud. But I cannot say it to her so this ink is wasted."

It is the next night and, despite my dismissal of its worth, I take up my pen and ink again. I open the book. The first page is blank. My memory of writing on the page is clear but the page is blank. Is my memory lying to me?
"Dear Diary,
Today on the bus I wanted to curse, to shout obscenities and bare myself to passing traffic. There are those who do of course but where does it get them? They wake up alone and poor."

It is the next night and the page is blank again. Is the ink fading?
"Dear Diary, I am scared. Imagine saying that to a colleague. "Mr.Barton, I am scared." Imagine his horror, his embarrassment. Tomorrow I will whisper it to his back."

It is the next night. The page is blank. I count the pages: 362. The pages are disappearing. Someone must be stealing the pages. I begin to construct elaborate scenarios from my suspicions. Who would want to know my secret thoughts? But had I not once wished to see inside Brenda's diary? If I had spied it when visiting her in her flat and she had left the room briefly to make a cup of tea would I not have been tempted to steal a glance at a few words? Would I then not have been tempted to construct possible elaborations of the words? But it would have been my own hopes and fears that I would have read there. From this confession dear Diary I deduce that the pages could have been stolen by absolutely anyone.
I expect, as I expect sunrise, that in the morning this page will have disappeared.

The sun has risen. The page has gone.
I continue to write every night. My confessions become more honest, with the thought that they are being read. I am no longer scared of them being seen because they are evidently being read by someone who welcomes them, needs them, but this fantasy

does not last for my door is bolted from the inside at night and there are no windows in my flat.

Am I destroying the pages myself in my sleep? Is there a part of me that abhors these feelings; that would rather I was a perfect citizen with no feelings that needed to be hidden? I will stay at Brenda's tonight.

It is the next night. The page has gone. I will continue to write on these pages of water.

"Dear Diary,
The shops are wrong, they are not diaries. I do not write to them and it is not this book that I am writing to either. I am not addressing these paper pages or their plastic cover or the gum in their spine. Dear Diary, who are you?"

Water.

"Dear Diary,
I want to leave the city. What is outside the city? Is that where you reside? Do you have a throne on the other side of the world?"

Water.

I am hammering a chisel into the far wall of my flat, the end of the concrete ray. This is the culmination of my life so far. Bang follows bang with no lessening of passion. My desire grows as my energy fades. Bang. Bang. It falls away in chunks.

I can see a little light that grows.

The hole is big enough to crawl through.

I crawl through.

The ground is covered in pages, knee deep, as far as the horizon. White pages covered in writing in different hands lay naked, exposed, pressed against each other. It is overwhelming. I wade through them.

I walk in a straight line all day, bewildered but purposeful, towards Diary's throne.

As I near the world's opposite pole I see other people. They are striding from every direction towards the same destination, fearless with nothing to lose. Could it be that everyone has broken through their respective rays at the same time and for the same reason as I?

When we reach a distance where Diary's throne should be in sight we all realise that it is not there and that it is not the throne that we are walking towards but each other. The mass hallucination was a curtain that revealed a finer place. The air is full of speech.

We ran from each other to each other.
We now no longer live in the sun but are illuminated by it.
Now we become the throne.
Now we are Diary.

Terry Takes A Dip

Terry has decided to go for a dip in the ocean.
He stands on the shore and looks out to sea.
He steps into the water. His flesh that is beneath the water
immediately turns into tentacles, waving in the water. As he slowly
moves further out to sea, closer to whatever it is that he is seeking,
the tentacles grow longer until they are hanging from his waist. He
looks down at them dancing where his legs used to be, then he
moves still further out to sea until only his head is above the water.
Anyone seeing him from the beach would be able, if they knew
him, to recognise Terry but what strange creature had he become?
He is just a head with tentacles. Then they would see his head
disappear beneath the surface.

Now Terry is tentacles only, radiating from his centre, moving
deeper and deeper, feeling fish, feeling corral, feeling better and
better and better.

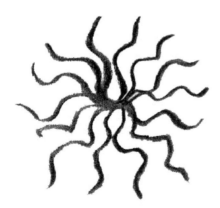

The Exit To Vince's Voyeurs' Emporium

Look through this keyhole and you will see Vince: a thin man with a thin moustache and large eyes. He is looking through a keyhole himself, crouched down outside his neighbour's door in the hallway between their rooms. The woman who lives behind the door undresses for bed at this time. Vince has never spoken to her. He watches her slide a finger between her knickers and her skin, stretching the elastic, then sliding the knickers down her legs...

"What if I were to break through this door", Vince thinks, "If my body softened and I squeezed through this keyhole to be with her...I would have to close my eyes to soften my dick. Then when I opened them again on the other side what if she spoke? I would not want her to speak."

Vince is the proprietor of "Vince's Voyeurs' Emporium (purveyors of gentlemen's literature)". He is returning from work but beyond his vision the porn store's walls grow to contain him. He walks through a graveyard.

"Beneath my feet are beautiful bodies", he thinks and puts a hand in a pocket, touching himself through the fabric, "Corpses unencumbered by feelings and thoughts, such a pity that they have to decay."

He is walking up the stairs to his room when he hears his neighbour's footsteps ascending the stairs behind him. He quickens his step, unlocks his door as fast as he can, rushes into the room then locks the door behind him. Breathing heavily, he crouches down and looks through the keyhole at the corridor. He sees her pass. He looks at his watch. One hour to wait. He stands then turns around, and stares at the wall that divides his flat from hers.

"I am in love with your corpse", he whispers, "You can throw away all of your feelings and thoughts, just give me a photograph of your tits. You can chuck out all of your hopes and your fears and evict all your dreams. Oh, your corpse, your beautiful husk, that skin, that fat. But I don't want decay, I don't want that beauty to rot, so you'll have to stick around, you'll have to stay alive but pretend that you're not there, stay silent and still. My darling living dead."

Vince is in his own depths now, with this honesty comes an opportunity. Beyond his vision an exit to the porn store appears then slowly takes on a visible form.

Vince turns around and begins to walk to the window but stops. There is a keyhole hovering in the middle of the room. It is floating impossibly. There is light coming from within it. Vince does not move. He stares at the keyhole, without moving, for two hours.

31

Vince shakes his head. The floating keyhole has caused him to miss the sight of his neighbour's naked body, now she will be sleeping in darkness. He curses then stares hard at the keyhole. He moves closer to it. He looks all around it, investigating for some hidden means of suspension but finds none. He bends closer, closes one eye, then with the other looks through the keyhole. He sees bright, white light. He shuts the briefly blinded eye, steps back, then slowly opens it again. The keyhole has changed. It is no longer a hole. It is solid and black, and the rest of the room is white light. The light is so bright that he can only look at the floating, solid, black, keyhole shaped object. The light slowly fades and he reaches out, grasps the floating object in his fist, and then opens his hand. The object sits upon his palm, no longer floating. He puts the object in his pocket, lies on his bed and sleeps, and dreams.

In the morning he awakes earlier than usual. He meets his neighbour in the corridor. He smiles at her and says, "Hello." She smiles back at him and says, "Hello."

Now he keeps the solid, black keyhole shaped object on his mantle piece.

Everything Is Fine

A family sings as they drive up to the huge gates of the sky blue dome of Happy World:
"We are off to Happy World where everything is fine,
We are off to Happy World where the sun always shines."

Inside Happy World, surrounded by smiling families playing games, a six foot teddy bear turns to a six foot duck and says:
"Urgh, God, get this fucking suit off me!"
"What?" says the duck.
"Get it off me! I've fucking shat myself! Why don't these costumes have arseholes?"
The duck starts laughing uncontrollably.
"Fuck you, I'm ill!" shouts the teddy bear.
Inquisitive children are beginning to gather around the teddy bear as he pulls at his fur.
"No arseholes, no cock and no heart. Why won't it unzip?"
"It's locked, man."
"What?"
"They're new suits, man, the boss has the key."
"What the fuck? Since when?"
"There was a memo this morning, man, new suits, they have keys so we don't nick them."
"Why the fuck would I want to nick a smiling teddy bear suit?"
"I don't know, man, maybe you're sick in the head as well as in the arse."
"Where's the boss?"
"Last time I saw him he was having some kid arrested in the tunnel of love for getting his dick out."
The teddy bear strides uncomfortably towards the tunnel of love.

"Boss! I got to get this suit off, I'm ill, I've err...defecated."
"Yes, I heard about your outburst, Ted."
"My name's not Ted."
The teddy bear's boss says nothing.
"Well, have you got the key?
"Yes."
"Well, are you going to let me out?"
"No."
"What?"
"You have a job to do."

"Are you kidding?"

"No."

The teddy bear lifts its paw ready to strike his boss then begins to dance. He skips, waltzes and pirouettes, shouting:

"What the fuck's going on?"

"We may get rid of you actors soon now that we have these mechanical suits," the teddy bear's boss says and presses a button on the remote control in his hand. The teddy bear turns and dances towards the gift shop. Children follow him, trying to hug him, trying to kiss him.

The gift shop has many rooms, the teddy bear dances through each one. The first is full of cuddly toys: furry, sexless, harmless creatures. The second is full of rubber fried-eggs, plastic lettuces and strings of foam sausages. The third is full of plastic faeces and rubber piles of vomit. The fourth is full of plastic severed arms and stick on scars. The teddy bear dances into a shelf full of bottles of fake blood and falls to the floor. The suit splits open and diarrhoea pours out. Lying on his back, the teddy bear's limbs dance on.

The teddy bear's boss looms over the teddy bear.

"Everything is fine inside Happy World," says the teddy bear's boss.

"No it is not. I know you," the teddy bear says, "You used to go up to children in the street and put clothes pegs on their cheeks to force them to smile. I am here to help you. I have waited for this moment. There is a place in your mind that wants you. It is a terrifying place, horrific but you must put your hand inside it and if you lie, lose your hand. You must hear what it has to say and you must fuck it. You must let it devour you and come out smiling. Look at my shit."

"Get out! Get out of here!" the teddy bear's boss shouts, "You are not welcome! You are a disease. You are evil. I can see evil's many faces before me. They are everywhere; they are everything I can see... Now they are converging and becoming a curtain... Now the curtain is opening... Now I am smiling. I can see behind the curtain. Why am I smiling? Oh help me. What is going on? Stop! I see people having sex and I am smiling. What have you done to me? It is an orgy. Now they are torturing each other and still I am smiling! My smile is disembodied now! It has left my face. I am watching it. It is too wide, too happy. It is insane. It is over there in the corner," the teddy bear's boss points, "It is smiling wider and wider, it is growing in length, revealing more and more teeth. It is making a sound as it grows, a high pitched "Heeeeeeeeeeeeeeeeeeeeeeeeeeeeeeeeeee......"

Now I am gripping it in my fist and whipping it against the floor, it is over a meter long. Now I am forcing it into a wicker hamper where it writhes and coils inside, still growing, still smiling. Still making that sound. Now it has forced the lid open and it is writhing over the sides."

"Everything is fine outside Happy World", the teddy bear says.

"No it is not! Hide your shit!"

"Shit is O.K. Everything is fine."

"But that smile will smile at me if I am alive or if I am dead or if I am good or if I am bad."

"It is love."

"Love?"

The teddy bear's boss's face changes.

The teddy bear's boss tentatively takes a step towards the wicker hamper and touches the smile. He lets it coil around his arm. The teddy bear and his boss grin as the smile grows to encompass everything and the ends of the smile meet.

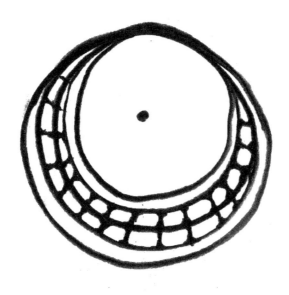

Up!

Space. Stars. Some are living now; some are dead now but all are shining bright, piercingly bright. They pierced me as I lay on my back in the garden with my hands beneath my head, propping it up from the ground.

Space.

I walked home from school with my tie in my pocket and my top button undone and swung my heavy satchel, enjoying the feeling of it levitating and weightless in the moment that it was at its highest. I swung it again and again, back and forth, until I reached the zebra crossing, then stood waiting for the cars to stop.

The weight of the satchel pulled on my hand. It pulled my hand towards the ground. Then the bad feeling happened. Pressure pushed down on me from above and I sunk. Down, down, down. Falling, obeying, sinking. I dropped to my knees and my head fell and pressed against the ground.

Someone tried to lift me but they couldn't, nobody could until the bad feeling allowed them to, until it went away. Then someone, a woman, said:

"Are you all right?"

And I said:

"Yes I am now, thankyou."

"Do you want me to drive you home?"

"No thankyou. I can walk."

"But you should see a doctor."

"Doctors can't stop it. It isn't a germ; it's just a bad feeling. It's gone now."

I walked home and threw my satchel up in the air again and again. I caught it every time!

Back home in my den I opened my rocket book and looked at the pictures.

I was in a competition today. It was at another school but I beat them. I came first! I can always jump the highest. I don't know how I do it, it's just something I can do. It's good because when I get things wrong the teacher doesn't pick on me like other people, I guess he thinks oh well at least he can jump the highest. It's not fair but there you are.

36

I saw five shooting stars tonight! Five! I couldn't think of a wish for the fifth one so I said my first wish again. So double probability of that coming true although I'm not sure if it works that way...Yeah, of course it does!

I don't know what it is. The bad feeling, I mean. It's always been here. It's scary.

I went to the tip today and found the biggest spring in the universe! It was taller than me! Mr Toby said I could have it!
  "You're a funny one," he said, "It's no use to me."
  "Thanks Mr Toby!"
  "How have you been this week?" he said.
  "It happened again," I said, "What do you think it is?"
  "I don't know, I don't think about it and neither should you. Don't give it the time of day. You keep thinking about your galaxies and planets, wonder about those instead."
  "O.K. Mr Toby."
  "Do you know the names of all the planets?"
  "Mercury, Venus, Earth, Mars, Jupiter, Saturn, Uranus, Neptune, Pluto."
  Mr Toby smiled. His lips went right up at the corners, defying the force that was always trying to push them flat.
  I dragged the spring home and put it in the shed with all the other things that I've collected."

The branch wasn't that high, I knew that I could jump it.
  "Come on then, if you're such a great jumper," said one boy.
  "Easy!" I said and ran towards the branch. Hup! No problem. Then down, but down further and further, falling, falling, further than I'd been before, pressure pushing down from above, my feet being sucked, dragged down and down. There was a hole in the ground on the other side of the branch. I didn't break any bones but the shock brought on the bad feeling. Down. To top it all there was a dead bird in the hole. Completely dead. My head pressed against the ground.
  The other boys ran off, scared.
  Night came.
  I was frightened. You would have been if you had been me and if you had felt how I had felt. Down.
  After a long time the bad feeling softened a little and I could just lift my head. Trees blocked out the stars and the sky. I think it was cloudy too.
  "Keep thinking about your galaxies and planets, wonder about them instead," I remembered so I did.

The bad feeling was still with me but not so heavy. I pushed against it and slowly managed to lift myself out of the hole. I crawled through the woods then down the street to my house but I didn't go in, I crawled around the back, into the garden and towards the shed. It was difficult but I managed to raise one hand and opened the shed door. I crawled inside. I found some string and tied all the things that I had collected to my feet then crawled out of the shed, dragging them behind me. The next bit was the hardest but I did it. I pulled myself up onto the shed roof. When I was up there I couldn't crawl anymore because the bad feeling was getting stronger again. I had to slide around on my stomach like a snake but still I managed to set it all up. I untied the things and fitted them all together. I had planned it so many times that building it was easy. When it was ready I rolled over onto my back and slid into position, on top of it, facing the stars. I held the knife in one hand and sawed through the rope. I've heard a few boings in my time but this was without doubt the biggest boing ever! And up I flew! Up, up, above the shed, above the house, above the town, towards the stars but then I turned my head and looked down at the world getting smaller and smaller and I thought about trees and animals and Mr Toby and I thought oh no what am I doing, do they have trees or animals or Mr Tobies in space? And then I was really scared but not for long because I turned my head back round and looked up at the stars growing bigger and bigger

as I shot into space, up and up and up and up and **up up up**

up up!

Brad's Quest

Brad is hopeful. He walks through a field, creating a pathway of trampled grass. His hope creates a pathway for me to fly through into the material world, allowing me to help him in his quest. I place a large rock in front of him, forcing him to turn and walk in another direction, gently nudging him towards his goal.

Brad walks into a forest.

He stops in front of a tree that has a carving on its bark and smiles. Above the carving he notices a rock balanced on a branch. The carving depicts the shape of the rock. He examines the rock and finds traces of bark on its sharp edge. He notes that the rock was used to create the carving of the rock.

"A clue", he thinks, "But what sort of a clue is this? It points only to itself. It is circular."

He walks on, deeper into the forest as the day turns to night. He sleeps inside a hollow tree trunk with hope in his heart. I fly through his hope into his dreams and he meets me there.

Brad wakes, smiles, stands up then walks on, continuing his search.

He finds another carving on another tree. He notes that it is identical to the first and that above it is an identical rock on an identical branch.

He walks on and sees a tree stump. He looks at the concentric circles of grain and realises that the second clue *was* the first clue. He has been circling. This does not upset him, in fact he smiles, hopeful that this realisation is a clue in itself. I travel through his hope and enter the body of a chicken. Through the chicken's eyes I spy Brad. I speak through the chicken.

Brad hears the chicken cluck and turns in its direction.

I walk the chicken away from Brad, into a thicket of bracken, still calling. Brad follows the chicken's clucking. He sees a tree stump. He looks at the grain. In place of concentric circles is a spiral. He traces it with a finger and smiles.

"Curious", he says.

The chicken clucks and Brad follows the noise again. He walks into a clearing and sees a great number of chickens pecking the ground, all clucking in front of a small brick house with smoke curling from its chimney and a green door. In the middle of the door is a small shelf upon which is a rock. Around the rock and the shelf is a carving in the shape of the rock. The rock has traces of green paint on its sharp edge. The door opens and out walks a girl carrying a shotgun.

"Who are you?" she shouts and my brother crawls and slithers through the tunnel of her fear, casts his invisible shadow over her chickens and one shrieks than dies. Her expression changes and she lowers her gun.

"Who are you?" she smiles and I fly through her smile, cast my invisible light upon her chickens and one lays an egg.

"My name is Brad. I am a detective."

The girl raises her gun again. Another chicken dies.

"What are you searching for?" she shouts.

"It's top secret."

"Don't you trust me?"

"You misunderstand. It's so top secret even *I* don't know."

She puts down her gun. A chicken lays an egg.

"It's cold out here. It's warm in my house. My name is Mary. Come into my house."

They enter the house.

"Do you prefer chickens or eggs?" she asks.

"I like both."

"Good."

She cooks him a dinner of roast chicken and fried eggs.

"I know what *I* am searching for", Mary says.

"What's that?" Brad asks between mouthfuls.

"Come with me."

Mary leads Brad by the hand. Outside, behind the house, is a small pile of straw surrounded by a fence.

"I had to build a fence because some of the chickens tried to attack it, out of fear I think. It's strange how some of them are scared of it and some are curious."

Sitting on the straw is a creature part chicken, part egg. It has a shell and a beak.

"Is it alive?" Brad asks.

"Yes, it opens its beak when it's hungry but I don't think it will live for very long", a terrible sadness appears in her face, "I don't know where it's from, I don't know how it got here. It's like me. I don't know where I am from. I am searching for my mother."

They turn, walk back into the house and sit by the fire.

"I see things", Mary says.

"What things?" Brad asks.

"Everyone already knows the answer to every question. It is within each of us but we cannot see it."

"Then your mother is somewhere inside you. Look inside yourself to find her."

"I can only look inside others."

"Then you can look inside me to find what I am searching for?"

"Yes."

Mary places a hand on Brad's forehead.

40

"I can feel it", she says.
She closes her eyes.
"I can see it", she says.
"What is it?" Brad says.
"I cannot tell you."
"Why?"
"You are not allowed to know."
They sit in silence then suddenly they are kissing. Whilst they make love on the floor Mary wonders where the first kiss began.

"Did I like him because he liked me?" she thinks, "Or did he like me because I liked him. Who made the first move? Where did our love begin, where did it come from?"

"I am pregnant," Mary says.
Brad smiles.
"That's wonderful!" he says.
"Aren't you scared?"
"What good would that do? Are you scared?"
"Sometimes I am full of fear, sometimes I am full of hope. Do I choose whether to hope or fear? Where does it begin? Where does it come from?"
"I don't know."
"The answer to your quest is inside *me* now", Mary says.
Brad raises his eyebrows then smiles.
"So now you have two answers inside you", he says.

Brad places a hand on Mary's large, round belly.
"I can feel something", he says.

In a hospital a nurse points at a monitor screen. On the screen is an ultrasound image of Brad and Mary's child.
"Look", the nurse says, "It's a girl."
Brad and Mary smile.

Whilst Brad and Mary sleep two nurses peer at the monitor screen.
"It *is* holding something!"
"I've never seen anything so frightening in all my life. What the hell is it?"
"I think it's wonderful! What could it be? It's so exciting!"
"Turn it off, I don't want to think about it."

"I can see her", Brad shouts, smiling as Mary screams.
As Brad cuts the umbilical cord he notices something clenched in the baby's fist. He gently prises her tiny fingers open to reveal a small transparent box smeared with blood.

Mary takes the baby in her arms, holds her to her bosom and places a hand on the baby's forehead.

"I can feel who you are," Mary says.

She closes her eyes.

"I can see who you are. Oh, Mother, it's you," Mary says, "Oh Mummy, Mummy."

Brad smiles. He wipes some of the blood from the transparent box and sees that it has a transparent lock. He wipes away the rest of the blood and sees that inside the box is a transparent key. He tries to open the box but it is locked. He shows it to Mary.

"I have seen it before", she says.

Brad kisses Mary and her mother; he smiles and I fly through his smile and whisper "Listen" in his ear. Brad hears a knocking sound, turns around and opens a door. There is nobody there. He peers into a blood red room. The knocking is louder: a deep, pulsing beat. He enters the room and the door closes behind him. He examines the walls, they are wet and they are living, pulsating in time with the beat. He suddenly feels as if something has entered his body and is residing in his heart. He walks around and the thing inside him moves. He stops and it stops. He looks about him.

"I am inside myself", he says, smiling, "How curious."

The walls around him begin to decay and the air becomes full of the stench of rotting meat. The room rots then crumbles to dust around his feet, leaving Brad holding the transparent locked box with a key inside it, standing in an infinite void. Brad feels no fear; he wonders at his situation and hopes that the box is what he was searching for. I fly through his hope and stand before him. He hands the box to me.

"The key inside the box unlocks the box", I say.

Brad smiles, is filled with complete understanding then becomes me. He flies through Brad's hope into the material world and places a large rock in front of him, forcing him to turn and walk in another direction, gently nudging him towards his goal.

The Miracle

In an underground room a man dressed in a white robe is reciting a legend:

"Somewhere, sometime, people were different. Once, when people were hurt they would secrete a transparent fluid from their eyes. Their eyes would rain. Each tried to prevent the others' eyes from raining, not by damming them or by cutting them out but by trying to prevent anything happening that might cause eyes to rain. Although this was an impossible task, they tried because they thought that it mattered."

Imagine a girl. Imagine a car. Imagine how the two may combine. The girl could be inside the car in various positions or on top of the car like in an advertisement. Or the two could be sliced and shuffled together, minced, mangled, mixed. The combinations are numerous. Imagine what the girl could do to the car. Imagine what the car could do to the girl. Some of these imaginings might seem to be shocking, perverse even, but such feelings are merely subjective and after all we are only talking about a car and a girl.

A little blonde girl called Sandy is playing with a doll and a toy car on a yellow carpet. The doll has been moulded from plastic, including its clothes; it is a hollow shell. Its face has been printed with a fixed, cheery grin. The car is much larger than the doll. The toys were not meant to be combined.

Sandy stands the doll on the carpet. It grins. Sandy pushes the car towards the doll. It still grins. Sandy is kneeling on the floor and bending over the toys, her face looms over them, grinning. The car moves towards the doll. Sandy makes the noise of the car's engine then the car hits the doll which continues to grin as does Sandy who then bashes the car against the doll until the doll breaks.

Sandy's mother has been watching her daughter with indifference.

Sandra Grace is walking across a zebra crossing. She is carrying a bag over her shoulder. Suddenly a car races towards her, strikes her, then continues on its way without stopping or even slowing. Sandra lies dead on the road. Her bag has split open revealing a white robe that the wind is now blowing, billowing across the street. Her body has also split open, causing a passer-by to shout:

"Ugh! You bitch! Look at my suit! Keep your blood to yourself!"

The body remains where it is until another car races towards it and is unable to drive over the obstacle however much the driver tries. The car reverses then accelerates forwards repeatedly but the wheels simply push the body further down the road and are unable to ride over it. The driver stops his car, curses that he is now late for an important business meeting then calls the police on his mobile phone.

The police officer who eventually arrives at the scene is called Stan. Stan walks over to the body, gives it a kick then says:

"There goes my early night, bitch."

Sandy has now abandoned her toys and is sitting in front of the television which is showing an image of a laboratory whilst an authoritative, male voice speaks:

"Everything which can be done is, has or will be done."

In the middle of the laboratory, surrounded by chemical apparatus, are two metal chairs. One chair has a dog strapped into it. The dog has a monkey's head grafted to its neck. The other chair has a monkey strapped into it. The monkey has a dog's head grafted to its neck. Both creatures' necks have been shaved, allowing the stitches to be seen. Both creatures twitch and shake and shudder and quake. Their eyes stare wildly.

Sandy points at the two creatures then laughs and claps her hands.

Desmond Grace is sat in his office, staring at a sheet of paper printed with numbers that is lying in front of him on his desk. He is the managing director of a wallpaper company. One of their designs adorns the office walls: small, pastel pink mushroom-clouds evenly spaced upon a light blue background. It is very aesthetically pleasing. There is a knock at the door.

"Who is it?" shouts Desmond.

"Tea sir", comes the nervous reply.

A small, middle-aged woman enters the room carrying a cup and saucer with both hands. She walks to the desk and sets the cup and saucer down between her and the sheet of paper printed with numbers. Desmond does not look at her. She then stands still, her hands clasped tightly behind her back. Slowly Desmond raises his eyes from the sheet of paper and stares at her.

"What is it? I'm a busy man."

"Mr Grace, I am sorry to take up your time but I am afraid that I feel I must. I have been working for you for twenty-three years now, always conscientiously..."

It is clear to Desmond that the speech has been memorised.

"...And I am proud to have done so. I have a large family: six children and I am without a husband. Five of my children are disabled and I have to pay for carers to look after them. I have recently discovered that I have cancer and so I am trying to save enough money to pay for their keep when I am gone. It was very kind of you to employ Susanna, especially as she is only nine but if I could just have a small pay increase of..."

Desmond interrupts aggressively:

"We all have an equal chance in life. There are winners and losers. Your problems are your problems, no one else's. I run a business. Do you understand? Now get out before you embarrass yourself further. I find your sense of self worth and preoccupation with your family's welfare utterly abhorrent. Get out!"

The woman turns and leaves.

"Honestly", mutters Desmond and begins to sip his tea. There is another knock at the door.

"What now?"

Stan, the police officer, enters the room.

"Mr Grace?" Stan asks.

"Yes?"

"Your daughter is dead."

Stan is renowned for his economy of language, his unwavering adherence to the facts, so much so that rumours of promotion have been circling him for some time.

"Oh fucking hell!" shouts Desmond, "It's just one thing after another, I'm never going to finish reading these numbers."

He sips his tea then enquires:

"How did she die?"

"She was knocked down by a car."

"Stupid bitch", says Desmond, "She was always day-dreaming."

"You are required to identify the body as soon as possible."

"Oh for fuck's sake. Right, come on then", he stands up to leave but the telephone on his desk rings. He picks it up.

"Yes?" he snaps.

"Hello Mr Grace. Do you know where Sandra is? There is no answer at her house."

"She's dead."

"Oh, right, thankyou, goodbye."

Desmond slams the receiver down then the two men leave the office.

In an underground room a man dressed in a white robe puts down his telephone receiver. He is The High Priest of the House of The Human Clouds. He turns to face a number of similarly dressed people and says:

45

"Sandra is dead."

The men and women look at each other with blank expressions.

"We must meditate on her death", The High Priest says, "Perhaps Sandra is our saviour."

The brothers and sisters of The House of the Human Clouds stand in a circle around The High Priest and hold hands. From a pocket inside his robe The High Priest produces a glass bottle and a cork. The brothers and sisters all think about Sandra. They think about her death and they search for the tragedy of the situation. They try to see Sandra as something more than an insignificant cog in a social machine; as something more than expendable and they try to see her death as something more than a meaningless random occurrence. Each of them concentrates.

"We will wring out the stone", they chant.

The High Priest approaches one of the members of the circle and holds the glass bottle under one of her eyes. He stares hard into that eye, searching for just a single drop of liquid, but finds nothing. He moves the bottle to beneath the other eye. His other hand holds the cork, poised, ready to trap the sacred prize. He moves slowly around the inside of the circle, from eye to eye. The bottle remains empty.

Desmond Grace and Stan look at the female corpse that Harry the mortuary attendant has slid from a wall of numbered drawers that look like elongated filing cabinets.

"Yes it is my daughter", Desmond says.

He looks at the corpse's face and slowly begins to feel...odd, somehow...out of place with the world. Turning to face Stan and Harry who are admiring the corpse's legs, he fights to retain his balance and says:

"I am leaving now. I am a busy man", then strides out of the building.

He thinks that he must be ill and tries to identify its source. Is it in his body or in his mind? He cannot tell but it is growing and now he has to stand still. It is overwhelming. He looks at the people passing by and actually considers stopping one of them and asking for help but now the feeling is growing again and it is changing him. His mouth is curling down at the corners and his brows are frowning. He struggles against it. He feels as if he is slipping away.

"Is this death?" he thinks.

His pulse races, he sweats. Thoughts of Sandra fill his mind: useless, irrational thoughts. Something begins to well up in his eyes. His whole being seems to be turning into tiny droplets of liquid. He blinks.

"Are my eyes bleeding?" he thinks.

He touches the liquid that is now running down his cheeks. He looks at his hand. The liquid is transparent.

"What is happening to me?" he thinks.

He tries to speak but only makes small yelps and little moans. He stands motionless, helpless.

A substantial gathering has formed in front of him. All are watching his face, in wonder. Tears are like unicorns and dragons, surely. A number of people dressed in white robes approach. One of them rushes over with a glass bottle and a cork in his hands whilst the others lay flower wreaths at Desmond Grace's feet.

The morning paper shows a photograph of Desmond's contorted and dripping face. The headline reads:

"Person Cries!"

The text beneath the photograph reads:

"A man was found yesterday evening standing in Main Street with what appeared to be *tears* pouring from his eyes. Medical examinations have found no cause for the secretion. The House of the Human Clouds has claimed the occurrence to be a miracle and are calling for radical social changes to minimise secretions. Experts suspect that the whole episode is simply an elaborate hoax."

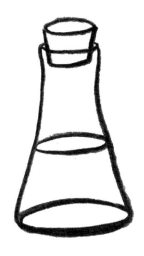

Wooden Globe

You do not see me. You see a woman standing in a wooden hallway. She is facing a wooden door. She knocks the door then waits, then knocks the door again then waits.

I do not see you. I do not see what you see. I do not see the woman facing the door. I see a forest. Inside the forest I see a tree-stump. I see an axe made of wood. I see a wooden hut. Inside the wooden hut I see a wooden wardrobe. Inside the wooden wardrobe I see a wooden man.

You do not see the forest. You see the woman facing the door, waiting. She knocks the door again then waits.

I see the forest grow. The wooden man cries wooden tears. He has a splinter in his thumb.

You see the woman facing the door hear a voice:
"You do not have to knock to *leave* the house."
"Oh," says the woman then opens the door and steps out.

We both see the woman walk into the forest. She sees a tree stump. She sees an axe made of wood. She sees a wooden hut. She enters the hut and sees a wooden wardrobe. She opens the wardrobe and sees the wooden man. The wooden man sees the woman and sees that she is made of wood.

We see for the first time that the air is also made of wood.
We see a wooden globe.

Love On The Other Side

The other side is where Daphne was walking towards when she walked to the corner shop last week to buy some soap. There was a man smoking a yellow pipe standing in her way. He was stood in the middle of the pavement in front of the corner shop.

"Excuse me," Daphne said.

The smoking man said nothing. He stared at Daphne with wild eyes, blew a plume of smoke from his mouth then laughed. Daphne pushed past him.

The other side is where Sylvester was walking towards when he walked to the corner shop yesterday to buy some plasters. He had cut himself whilst chopping wood for the fire. The smoking man was blocking his path, between Sylvester's bleeding cut and the plasters.

"Look," the smoking man said, "I'm turning to smoke," then laughed, "Just smoke."

Sylvester pushed past him.

Mr. Stracken, the owner of the corner shop, is the greatest poet that ever lived. Yet he has no knowledge of this and no one has ever read his poems. Autograph hunters do not follow him; paparazzi do not sleep in his porch. He keeps the poems in a shoebox beneath his bed. They will rot unseen. But his poems are famous on the other side, for they have changed this world beyond imagination; they have transformed life silently, insidiously.

The other side is where Sylvester is aiming for when he kisses Daphne and it's where Daphne is aiming for when she kisses Sylvester. It is because they were aiming for the other side that they met one another. They would like that to be known. They would like their love to be seen. They are to be married.

The night before their marriage Daphne and Sylvester both dream that the doorbell rings, that they get out of bed, that they wrap a dressing gown around them and answer the door. It is Mr. Stracken standing in his pyjamas.

"Love surrounded by fire inside a stone prayer," he says.

Daphne and Sylvester stand in a cathedral. Organ music surrounds them. A large congregation watches as they turn to face the altar. The altar is draped with red velvet. A gold candelabra stands in the altar's centre. The candle's flame flickers. A little smoke streams

from the flame's tip. A large book lies open beyond the candelabra.
The priest leads Daphne and Sylvester around to the other side of
the altar so that the candelabra is no longer between them and the
book. Daphne signs her name in the book then with the same pen
but different ink Sylvester signs his name beside it.

"You may kiss the bride," the priest says.

"Thankyou," Sylvester says.

Daphne grins and they wrap their arms around one another and
kiss. The congregation smiles many smiles.

Sylvester slides his tongue into Daphne's mouth as Daphne slides
her fingers through Sylvester's hair. Their hands wander all over
each other. Sylvester squeezes Daphne's breasts. Daphne moans
and pulls at Sylvester's trouser belt then undoes his zip.

The priest has become a statue of himself with a gaping mouth.

Daphne and Sylvester want their love to be seen. They turn it into
action and it changes their bodies, it hardens and lubricates them.

The cathedral is a prayer made of stone. The architect was aiming
for the other side when he designed it. He wanted that to be
known. He wanted his prayer to be seen.

"Can you see that my love is real?" Sylvester says to Daphne.

"Can you see that my love is real?" Daphne says to Sylvester.

"Can you see that our love is real?" Sylvester and Daphne say to
the priest and the congregation.

The members of the congregation have all developed a belated
interest in the intricate detail of late thirteenth century gothic
architecture; they are all staring intently at the cathedral's walls
and ceiling.

The statue of the priest has now become a part of the cathedral,
carved from the same stone.

Daphne and Sylvester are now rolling naked on the floor in front of
the altar. They become entangled in the red velvet drape,
obliviously tugging it rhythmically until the candelabra falls from the
altar, setting fire to the drape and burning the book. The fire
reanimates the priest.

"Stop, stop," he shouts, "The book! You are no longer in wedlock!"
Daphne and Sylvester continue to fuck.

"Fire! Fire!" the priest shouts.

Daphne, Sylvester, the congregation and the priest all catch alight.
Great plumes of smoke rise from the burning cathedral. Everyone
inside it dies. They all appear to turn to smoke.

Daphne and Sylvester can no longer be called by name. Something
deeper than feelings manifests itself as a dream. Like the priest-
statue's immobile mouth the spirits of Daphne and Sylvester can do

nothing but watch. The cathedral's architect's prayer appears to be nothing but smoke. Everything appears to be smoke. The spirits reach for the other side. They look through the smoke and become a question:

"Did we show our love to be real?"

The smoke becomes the many voices of the congregation. They speak at once but with different words:

"He just wanted your body."

"She just wanted your money."

"You were deceiving each other."

"You were deceiving yourselves."

Then with one accord the voices say:

"Murderers!"

Then all becomes smoke once again.

The spirits that are a question change. They stare at the smoke. They say:

"Could it have been love if it caused such destruction?"

The spirits examine the smoke. They trace its path back to its conception. They see an enormous yellow pipe. They hear laughter. The spirits push against the laughter. They question it. They say:

"Is all just smoke?"

The laughter parts, disperses and lets them pass through. Now the spirits can be named again.

On the other side it is night and Daphne and Sylvester are dressed in black. They stand outside a huge office block. Trying not to make a sound they try the door. It is open. They tiptoe inside. Sylvester shines a torch and illuminates a poster on the wall.

"Isn't that Mr. Stracken?" Daphne whispers, "Look, it says something underneath his photo...'Things that are not things cannot burn. On the other side those things are things'," she reads.

"We are on the right track," Sylvester says.

"Yes," Daphne smiles.

They are in a large room full of filing cabinets; each of the cabinets' drawers is printed with a year. Daphne and Sylvester walk past them until they come to "2002", the year that they fell in love. The drawer is not locked. Inside they flick through file cards printed with names until they come to one that reads:

"Daphne and Sylvester."

Beneath their name is printed a number:

"Four, nine, two, seven, one, three, five, eight, six."

They look at one another, shrug then close the drawer, taking the file card with them. They walk through the room and emerge into another. The room smells strongly of something strange and intoxicating. Sylvester shines the torch around them, illuminating thousands of shelves stacked with cardboard boxes. Each box is numbered. They search for the number on the file card.

Eventually they find it and between them manage to lift the box down from its shelf and carry it back through the room of filing cabinets, out of the building and into the street.

In their home Daphne and Sylvester kneel opposite one another on their double bed with the cardboard box between them. The top of the box is covered in dust, which Sylvester blows, turning it into a cloud that looks like smoke.

"What if it is empty?" Sylvester says and looks at Daphne.

"Then we part."

"Yes."

"Open it."

Sylvester reaches through the smoke-like dust cloud and opens the box. They both peer inside. Euphoria engulfs them. They reach inside and lift the box's contents out, sitting it on the bed between them and discarding the cardboard box. They grin and laugh and hug and kiss.

On the bed, between them, is their love. It is beautiful, colourful, soft in places, hard in others, glowing, pulsating, tentacles waving, petals and wings opening. They touch it, feeling its cavities and protrusions. It makes a sound like music. They cuddle it and stroke it and fondle it and lick it and kiss it.

Carefully, they lift it between them and stand in front of the window, holding it aloft and smiling. Down in the street the priest and the congregation look up and cheer.